Mr. Bear
to the Rescue

DEBI GLIORI

SCHOLASTIC INC.

New York Toronto London Auckland Sydney
Mexico City New Delhi Hong Kong Buenos Aires

For all those Mr. Bears:
Guri and Kari, Gay and Michael,
Ben, Sophie and Patrick,
my very dear Kirsty,
Belinda and Lyndsay,
Jaca and Judy,
but most of all,
for you.
You.

ISBN 0-439-37557-6

12 11 10 9 8 7 6 5 4 3 2 1   1 2 3 4 5 6/0

Printed in the U.S.A.   24

First Scholastic printing, December 2001

The text of this book is set in 16 point Veljovic Medium.
The illustrations are watercolor.

Book design by Nancy Goldenberg

It was a wild and windy night in the forest—
the kind of night where the best place to be was
in bed, snug and warm, with windows and
doors tightly shut.

Mr. Bear was tucked up in bed, while outside the wind was shaking the windows and howling down the chimney, trying to get in.

"What was that noise?" said Mrs. Bear, sitting up.

"Just the wind, dear," said Mr. Bear.

"I thought I heard a voice calling *Help!*" said Mrs. Bear.

"Help!" said a small voice.

"There," said Mrs. Bear. "I did hear a voice. Could you go and see who it is, dear?"

Mr. Bear obediently went downstairs.
As he opened the front door, a blast of wind
blew out his candle and peppered him
with fallen leaves.

"Please help," said a very small voice
from somewhere around Mr. Bear's ankles.

Clinging to Mr. Bear's doorstep
was Mr. Rabbit-Bunn. "Our warren has
collapsed," he wailed. "The Hoot-Toowits'
nest has blown away, the Buzzes' hive
is ruined, and I have to go back because
we can't find baby Flora *anywhere.*"

And with that, Mr. Rabbit-Bunn ran off
into the night.

"Help is on its way," said Mr. Bear, lighting a lantern. He packed some tools and grabbed a honey sandwich, just in case.

"Do be careful, dear," called Mrs. Bear, as Mr. Bear was blown down the garden path.

"Don't worry," said Mr. Bear, feeling very worried indeed. "I'll be fine."

It was a long way to the Rabbit-Bunns' house.
Mr. Bear tripped and stumbled over fallen branches, and
several times his lantern nearly blew out.

I wish I was back in my warm bed, thought Mr. Bear.
Icy rain blew into Mr. Bear's face as he struggled uphill.
"Just a little farther," said Mr. Bear to encourage himself.

A tangle of feathers and claws blew into
Mr. Bear's face. "Aaaaaargh!" he shrieked.
"Eeeek!" squawked Mr. Hoot-Toowit.
"Oh, it's *you*!" they both cried.
Mr. Bear struggled to his feet
and peered into the darkness.
"I can't see your house
anywhere," he said.

"You're standing in it,"
said Mr. Hoot-Toowit sadly.
"Goodness, so I am," said Mr. Bear.
There, all around, lay the battered remains of
the tree that Mr. Hoot-Toowit had shared with his
family, the Buzz family, and the Rabbit-Bunns.

"Oh, Mr. Bear, thank heavens you've come," cried a voice.
"Can you help us find Flora?"
"And can you fix our hive?"
"And mend our nest?"

Instantly Mr. Bear was surrounded
by rabbits and owls and bees, all
beseeching him for help.

Help? thought Mr. Bear. *What
on earth am I supposed to do?* He
scrambled around his tool kit and
found the honey sandwich that he'd
thrown in there as he left his house.

A brilliant idea occurred to him.

"What's that for?" asked one of the small Rabbit-Bunns.

"Glue," said Mr. Bear, peeling the sandwich apart. "Hive glue, in fact. Look, I'll spread a little bit here and another dollop there and—"

"End up with a sticky mess," groaned a small Buzz.

"Oh dear," said Mr. Bear, "let's take the hive home for Mrs. Bear to fix. She's very good at that sort of thing."

"What about my nest?" said Mr. Hoot-Toowit.

"I'll just have a look," said Mr. Bear, picking it up. The nest fell apart in his paws. Mrs. Hoot-Toowit sighed.

"Ah," said Mr. Bear. "Mrs. Bear'll knit you another in no time."

As the animals put the sticky hive and broken nest
into Mr. Bear's tool kit, the heavens opened up.

Rain poured down through the trees, seeking out anything that was dry and instantly turning it cold and soggy. The animals ran for shelter.

Mr. Bear's lantern hissed, fizzled, and went out.

"How will we ever find Flora now?" wailed Mrs. Rabbit-Bunn.

"Mr. Bear looked up at the sky anxiously. "Good grief," he said.

"What's that?" said Mr. Hoot-Toowit through a mouthful of twigs.

"I've found Flora!" yelled Mr. Bear, pointing upward. There, high in the branches of the sheltering tree, was a small rabbit, still wrapped in a blanket and fast asleep.

"I'll just climb up there
and get her," said Mr. Bear.
"What a hero you are," sighed
Mrs. Rabbit-Bunn.
Mr. Bear did not feel heroic
as he inched up the tree.

The slippery, rain-soaked branches gave out alarming groans and creaks as he grabbed them.

Mr. Bear disentangled the blanket from the branch, cradled Flora in his arms, and . . .

"Aaaargh!" yelled Mr. Bear.
"Wheeeeee!" cried Flora, waking up.
"Gosh, what a good idea," said Mr. Rabbit-Bunn, as Flora's blanket fanned out into a perfect parachute and Mr. Bear and the bunny floated safely to the ground.

"What a brilliant Mr. Bear!" said Mrs. Rabbit-Bunn,
hugging Mr. Bear's knees.

"Let's get these children tucked into bed,"
said Mr. Bear, loading the Rabbit-Bunns, Buzzes,
and Hoot-Toowits into his tool kit.

"It's very dark," said Mr. Hoot-Toowit.

"I can't see," wailed a small Rabbit-Bunn.

Neither can I, thought Mr. Bear, pushing his heavy tool kit to the top of a hill. But there, off in the distance, was his house with all the lights on, shining through the darkness.

"Hold on tight," he said. "We're nearly home."

Much later, when towels and blankets had been found for everyone, and Mrs. Bear's hot nettle soup had warmed every tummy, large and small, the Bear house filled with snores from the Buzzes, the Hoot-Toowits, and the Rabbit-Bunns.

Baby Bear clambered up Mr. Bear's leg.
Mr. Bear sank into a chair with a groan.
   Mrs. Bear looked up from her nest-knitting with
a mischievous smile. "What a brilliant Mr. Bear your
daddy is," she said. "So good at fixing things."
   Mr. Bear gave a huge yawn.

"In fact," continued Mrs. Bear, "there are a few things around here that need fixing by that daddy. There's the squeaky bathroom door, the blocked sink, and the smoky chimney . . ."

Mr. Bear gave a loud snore.

". . . but they can all wait till tomorrow," said Mrs. Bear, fetching a warm blanket for Mr. Bear and Baby Bear. "Even brilliant Mr. Bears need to be tucked in at times," she said. And she blew out the candles and headed upstairs to bed.